Defoe Abbott Marx Hardy Montaigne Machiavelli Chesterton Cooper Emerson Joyce Austen
Melville Haggard Hugo Grimm
Stoker Christie Carroll Eliot Molière
Wilde Maupassant Byron Schiller
Garnett Einstein Fitzgerald Engels Hawthorne Smith Kafka
Goethe Dostoyevsky Hall
Cotton Kipling Doyle Willis
Baum Henry Nietzsche
Leslie Dumas Flaubert Turgenev Balzac
Stockton Vatsyayana Crane
Burroughs Verne
Curtis Tocqueville Gogol Vinci
Homer Widger Tolstoy Whitman Busch
Darwin Thoreau Twain
Potter Freud Zola Scott
Kant Jowett Stevenson Dickens Plato Harte
Andersen Hesse
London Descartes Cervantes Burton
Poe Aristotle Wells Voltaire
Hale James Hastings Cooke
Bunner Shakespeare Irving
Richter Chekhov Chambers Alcott
Doré Dante da Shaw Wodehouse Benedict
Swift Pushkin Newton

tredition was established in 2006 by Sandra Latusseck and Soenke Schulz. Based in Hamburg, Germany, tredition offers publishing solutions to authors and publishing houses, combined with world-wide distribution of printed and digital book content. tredition is uniquely positioned to enable authors and publishing houses to create books on their own terms and without conventional manu-facturing risks.

For more information please visit: www.tredition.com

TREDITION CLASSICS

This book is part of the TREDITION CLASSICS series. The creators of this series are united by passion for literature and driven by the intention of making all public domain books available in printed format again - worldwide. Most TREDITION CLASSICS titles have been out of print and off the bookstore shelves for decades. At tredition we believe that a great book never goes out of style and that its value is eternal. Several mostly non-profit literature projects provide content to tredition. To support their good work, tredition donates a portion of the proceeds from each sold copy. As a reader of a TREDITION CLASSICS book, you support our mission to save many of the amazing works of world literature from oblivion. See all available books at www.tredition.com.

 Project Gutenberg

The content for this book has been graciously provided by Project Gutenberg. Project Gutenberg is a non-profit organization founded by Michael Hart in 1971 at the University of Illinois. The mission of Project Gutenberg is simple: To encourage the creation and distribution of eBooks. Project Gutenberg is the first and largest collection of public domain eBooks.

Poems

Elizabeth Stoddard

Imprint

This book is part of TREDITION CLASSICS

Author: Elizabeth Stoddard
Cover design: Buchgut, Berlin – Germany

Publisher: tredition GmbH, Hamburg - Germany
ISBN: 978-3-8424-5030-1

www.tredition.com
www.tredition.de

Copyright:
The content of this book is sourced from the public domain.

The intention of the TREDITION CLASSICS series is to make world literature in the public domain available in printed format. Literary enthusiasts and organizations, such as Project Gutenberg, world-wide have scanned and digitally edited the original texts. tredition has subsequently formatted and redesigned the content into a modern reading layout. Therefore, we cannot guarantee the exact reproduction of the original format of a particular historic edition. Please also note that no modifications have been made to the spelling, therefore it may differ from the orthography used today.

POEMS

BY

ELIZABETH STODDARD

1895

CONTENTS

POEMS

THE POET'S SECRET.

The poet's secret I must know,
If that will calm my restless mind.
I hail the seasons as they go,
I woo the sunshine, brave the wind.

I scan the lily and the rose,
I nod to every nodding tree,
I follow every stream that flows,
And wait beside the steadfast sea.

I question melancholy eyes,
I touch the lips of women fair:
Their lips and eyes may make me wise,
But what I seek for is not there.

In vain I watch the day and night,
In vain the world through space may roll:
I never see the mystic light
Which fills the poet's happy soul.

Through life I hear the rhythmic flow
Whose meaning into song must turn;
Revealing all he longs to know,
The secret each alone must learn.

NOVEMBER.

Much have I spoken of the faded leaf;

Long have I listened to the wailing wind,
And watched it ploughing through the heavy clouds,
For autumn charms my melancholy mind.

When autumn comes, the poets sing a dirge:
The year must perish; all the flowers are dead;
The sheaves are gathered; and the mottled quail
Runs in the stubble, but the lark has fled!

Still, autumn ushers in the Christmas cheer,
The holly-berries and the ivy-tree:
They weave a chaplet for the Old Year's bier
These waiting mourners do not sing for me!

I find sweet peace in depths of autumn woods.
Where grow the ragged ferns and roughened moss;
The naked, silent trees have taught me this, —
The loss of beauty is not always loss!

MUSIC IN A CROWD.

When I hear music, whether waltz or psalm,
Among a crowd, I find myself alone;
It does not touch me with a soothing balm,
But brings an echo like a moan

From some far country where a palace rose,
In which I reigned with Cleopatra's pride:
"Come, Charmian! bring the asp for my repose."
And queenly, men shall say, she died.

There lived and ruled a happy, noble race,
Primeval souls who held imperial power —
My kindred, gone forever from their place,
And I am here without a dower!

They were a Vision, though. And are these real,
These men and women, moving as in sleep,
Who, smiling, gesture to the same Ideal,
For which the music makes me weep?

Have they my longings for that other world
New to them yet? I grant that Music's swell
Is like the sea; they may be thither hurled
By storms that thunder and compel;

Or, like those voyagers in the land of streams,
Glide through its languid air, its languid wave,
To learn that *Here* and *There* are but two dreams,
That end in Nothing and the Grave!

"I LIVE WITHIN THE STRANGER'S GATE."

I.

I live within the stranger's gate,
And count the hours
Since God let fall the bolt of fate!
Where the waves fall on yonder shore
In cloudy spray,
And where the winds forever roar,
The pillars of a mansion stand,
Without a roof;
The saddest ruin in the land!

II.

When sunset strikes across the sea
The wreck looms up;
Then Memory comes, and touches me.
I see a pitiful white face
Break through the mould

Decaying at the pillar's base,
And hands that beckon me to prayer.
But I still curse,
And wake the Furies slumbering there!

III.

In the strange drama of the Past
It was my part
To hold carousal to the last;
It was for me to hide the shame,
And brave the world
With lies about our ancient name!
I played it well, and played it long:
But let it pass,
The world has never known the 'wrong.

IV.

Upheave, black mould, and totter all
The ruin down!
Fall, monumental pillars, fall,
Upon her grave! Above her breast
May ivy creep,
And roses blow! I choose to rest.

THE HOUSE OF YOUTH.

The rough north winds have left their icy caves
To growl and grope for prey
Upon the murky sea;
The lonely sea-gull skims the sullen waves
All the gray winter day.

The mottled sand-bird runneth up and down,
Amongst the creaking sedge,

Along the crusted beach;
The time-stained houses of the sea-walled town
Seem tottering on its edge.

An ancient dwelling, in this ancient place,
Stands in a garden drear,
A wreck with other wrecks;
The Past is there, but no one sees a face
Within, from year to year.

The wiry rose-trees scratch the window-pane;
The window rattles loud;
The wind beats at the door,
But never gets an answer back again,
The silence is so proud.

The last that lived there was an evil man;
A child the last that died,
Upon the mother's breast.
It seemed to die by some mysterious ban;
Its grave is by the side

Of an old tree, whose notched and scanty leaves
Repeat the tale of woe,
And quiver day and night,
Till the snow cometh, and a cold shroud weaves,
Whiter than that below.

This time of year a woman wanders there—
They say from distant lands:
She wears a foreign dress,
With jewels on her breast, and her fair hair
In braided coils and bands.

The ancient dwelling and the garden drear
At night know something more:
Without her foreign dress
Or blazing gems, this woman stealeth near
The threshold of the door.

The shadow strikes against the window-pane;
She thrusts the thorns away:
Her eyes peer through the glass,
And down the glass her great tears drip, like rain,
In the gray winter day.

The moon shines down the dismal garden track,
And lights the little mound;
But when she ventures there,
The black and threatening branches wave her back,
And guard the ghostly ground.

What is the story of this buried Past?
Were all its doors flung wide,
For us to search its rooms,
And we to see the race, from first to last,
And how they lived and died: —

Still would it baffle and perplex the brain.
But show this bitter truth:
Man lives not in the past:
None but a woman ever comes again
Back to the House of Youth!

THE HOUSE BY THE SEA.

To-night I do the bidding of a ghost,
A ghost that knows my misery;
In the lone dark I hear his wailing boast,
"Now shalt thou speak with me."

Must I go back where all is desolate,
Where reigns the terror of a curse,
To knock, a beggar, at my father's gate,
That closed upon a hearse?

The old stone pier has crumbled in the sea;
The tide flows through the garden wall;
Where grew the lily, and where hummed the bee,
Black seaweeds rise and fall.

I see the empty nests beneath the eaves;
No bird is near; the vines have died;
The orchard trees have lost the joy of leaves,
The oaks their lordly pride.

Of what avail to set ajar the door
Through which, when ruin fell, I fled?
If on the threshold I should stand once more,
Shall I behold the dead?

Shall I behold, as on that fatal night,
My mother from the window start,
When she was blasted by the evil sight, —
The shame that broke her heart?

The yellow grass grows on my sister's grave;
Her room is dark — she is not there;
I feel the rain, and hear the wild wind rave —
My tears, and my despair.

A white-haired man is singing a sad song
Amid the ashes on the hearth;
"Ashes to ashes, I have moaned so long
I am alone on earth."

No more! no more! I cannot bear this pain;
Shut the foul annals of my race;
Accursed the hand that opens them again,
My dowry of disgrace.

And so, farewell, thou bitter, bitter ghost!
When morning comes the shadows fly;
Before we part, I give this merry toast, —

The dead that do not die!

CHRISTMAS COMES AGAIN.

Let me be merry now, 't is time;
The season is at hand
For Christmas rhyme and Christmas chime,
Close up, and form the band.

The winter fires still burn as bright,
The lamp-light is as clear,
And since the dead are out of sight,
What hinders Christmas cheer?

Why think or speak of that abyss
In which lies all my Past?
High festival I need not miss,
While song and jest shall last.

We'll clink and drink on Christmas Eve,
Our ghosts can feel no wrong;
They revelled ere they took their leave—
Hearken, my Soldier's Song:

"The morning air doth coldly pass,
Comrades, to the saddle spring:
The night more bitter cold will bring
Ere dying—ere dying.
Sweetheart, come, the parting glass;
Glass and sabre, clash, clash, clash,
Ere dying—ere dying.
Stirrup-cup and stirrup-kiss—
Do you hope the foe we'll miss,
Sweetheart, for this loving kiss,
Ere dying—ere dying?"

The feasts and revels of the year
Do ghosts remember long?
Even in memory come they here?
Listen, my Sailor's Song:

"O my hearties, yo heave ho!
Anchor's up in Jolly Bay—
Hey!
Pipes and swipes, hob and nob—
Hey!
Mermaid Bess and Dolphin Meg,
Paddle over Jolly Bay—
Hey!
Tars, haul in for Christmas Day,
For round the 'varsal deep we go;
Never church, never bell,
For to tell
Of Christmas Day.
Yo heave ho, my hearties O!
Haul in, mates, here we lay—
Hey!"

His sword is rusting in its sheath,
His flag furled on the wall;
We'll twine them with a holly-wreath,
With green leaves cover all.

So clink and drink when falls the eve;
But, comrades, hide from me
Their graves—I would not see them heave
Beside me, like the sea.

Let not my brothers come again,
As men dead in their prime;
Then hold my hands, forget my pain,
And strike the Christmas chime.

MARCH.

Ho, wind of March, speed over sea,
From mountains where the snows lie deep
The cruel glaciers threatening creep,
And witness this, my jubilee!

Roar from the surf of boreal isles,
Roar from the hidden, jagged steeps,
Where the destroyer never sleeps;
Ring through the iceberg's Gothic piles!

Voyage through space with your wild train,
Harping its shrillest, searching tone,
Or wailing deep its ancient moan,
And learn how impotent your reign.

Then hover by this garden bed,
With all your wilful power, behold,
Just breaking from the leafy mould,
My little primrose lift its head!

THE SPRING AFAR.

Far from the empire of my present days,
Where I perforce remain,
The wild, fresh airs of Spring blow to and fro,
Piping out Winter's reign.

I know the rosy wind-flowers spread like clouds
Above the leafy mould,
And pollard willows over shallow pools
Stretch out their rods of gold.

I hear the waters in the mossy swamps

Start on their ocean quest,
Gliding through meadows, murmuring in woods,
Till reaching final rest.

Fixed in my thoughts is Spring, so long remote,
Though Spring cannot endow
As Summer can, or yield sweet Autumn's peace:
'T is that my heart needs now;

Or hope—maybe that Spring and Hope are one.
Therefore I should not ask
For leave from this my place: *both* may be near,
Behind my daily mask.

WHY?

Why did I go where roses grew,
And meadow larks which skyward flew
From grasses sparkling in the dew,
The yellow sunshine pouring through?
What was there for me to find?
Were they to learn my froward mind?
From far across vast summer seas,
Rifling green marshes, bending trees,
Driving cloud-shadows down the air,
Keen breezes smote me here and there,
Keen breezes crying, *Why, why, why?*
And nothing had I to reply!
Beings with neither soul nor sense,
Convicting me with their pretence;
Beings of change,—but what am I,—
Once more repeating, *Why, why, why?*

AUGUST.

Read by the wayside, read by the brook,
That this is the passion of the year;
Look at the fields, look at the woods,
Look upon me, and — draw near!

Just as these days are, so is my heart;
Lilies are flaming, berries are ripe;
Alders blow sweet, acorns are full —
And the bobolink's young ones pipe!

Ponder the river, ponder the sky,
Hazy and gray, hazy and blue;
Study the trees wed to the wind —
I promise you I'll be as true!
Yes, true as August — as the birds' song,
The sweet fern's scent, the weedy, blue shore,
The shine of vines, smilax, and grape —
What can you ask for more?

OCTOBER.

Falling leaves and falling men!
When the snows of winter fall,
And the winds of winter blow,
Will be woven Nature's pall.

Let us, then, forsake our dead,
For the dead will surely wait,
While we rush upon the foe,
Eager for the hero's fate.

Leaves will come upon the trees,
Spring will show the happy race;
Mothers will give birth to sons,

Loyal souls to fill our place.

Wherefore should we rest and rust?
Soldiers, we must fight and save
Freedom now, and give our foes
All their country should—a grave!

"THE WILLOW BOUGHS ARE YELLOW NOW."

The willow boughs are yellow now,
For spring has come again;
The peach-tree buds begin to swell,
Dripping with April rain.

The gray-eyed twilight lingers long,
To meet the starry night;
I walk the darkening lanes alone,
And love the sombre light.

The dream of other days returns,
When comes the blossomed spring;
But when the full leaved summer comes
My dream has taken wing;

The twittering swallows in the lane
Were there a year ago;
The old nests in the tangled vines
Their next year's brood will know.

A little brood of children fair,
Under the mother's wing,
Is in the dream of other days,
That flies when flies the spring!

"IN THE STILL, STAR-LIT NIGHT."

In the still, star-lit night,
By the full fountain and the willow-tree,
I walked, and not alone —
A spirit walked with me!

A shade fell on the grass;
Upon the water fell a deeper shade:
Something the willow stirred,
For to and fro it swayed.

The grass was in a quiver,
The water trembled, and the willow-tree
Sighed softly; I sighed loud —
The spirit taunted me.

All the night long I walked
By the full fountain, dropping icy tears;
I tore the willow leaves,
I tore the long, green spears!

I clutched the quaking grass,
And beat the rough bark of the willow-tree;
I shook the wreathed boughs,
To make the spirit flee.

It haunted me till dawn,
By the full fountain and the willow-tree;
For with myself I walked —
How could the spirit flee?

AUTUMN.

No melancholy days are these!

Not where the maple changing stands,
Not in the shade of fluttering oaks,
Nor in the bands

Of twisting vines and sturdy shrubs,
Scarlet and yellow, green and brown,
Falling, or swinging on their stalks,
Is Sorrow's crown.

The sparkling fields of dewy grass,
Woodpaths and roadsides decked with flowers,
Starred asters and the goldenrod,
Date Autumn's hours.

The shining banks of snowy clouds,
Steadfast in the aerial blue,
The silent, shimmering, silver sea,
To Joy are true.

My spirit in this happy air
Can thus embrace the dying year,
And with it wrap me in a shroud
As bright and clear!

THE AUTUMN SHEAF.

Still I remember only autumn days,
When golden leaves were floating in the air,
And reddening oaks stood sombre in the haze,
Till sunset struck them with its redder glare,

And faded, leaving me by wood and field
In fragrant dew, and fragrant velvet mould,
To wait among the shades of night concealed,
And learn that story which but once is told.

Though many seasons of the falling leaves
I watched my failing hopes, and watched their fall;
In memory they are gathered now like sheaves,
So withered that a touch would scatter all.

Dead leaves, and dust more dead, to fall apart,
Leaves spreading once in arches over me,
And dust enclosing once a loving heart,
Still I am happy with youth's mystery.

It cannot be unbound, — my autumn sheaf;
So let it stand, the ruin of my past;
Returning autumn brings the old belief,
Its mystery all its own, and it will last.

IN THE CITY.

The autumn morning sweetly calls to me,
And autumn days and nights in patience wait;
I answer not, because I am not free,
Although I chose my fate.

The cold, gray mist that stains the city walls
Stands silver-columned where the river glides,
Or, slow dividing, on the valley falls,
Where one I love abides.

The wind that trifles round my city door,
Or whirls before me all the city's dust,
By the sea borrows its triumphant roar,
And lends its savage gust;

Or shrieking rushes where the sombre pines
Hold solemn converse in the ancient vale,
And while 't is dying in their dark confines
Babbles their mystic tale.

Could I but climb a roof above my own,
And greet grave Autumn as he walks the earth
With secret signal that would make me known,
I should not feel my dearth.

Then silver mist or loud triumphant wind
Might come in sad disguise and misery;
I would but ponder in my secret mind
How Autumn answers me.

"I LOVE YOU, BUT A SENSE OF PAIN."

I love you, but a sense of pain
Is in my heart and in my brain;
Now, when your voice and eyes are kind,
May I reveal my complex mind?

Though I am yours, it is my curse
Some ideal passion to rehearse:
I dream of one that's not like you,
Never of one that's half so true.

To quell these yearnings, vague and wild,
I often kneel by our dear child,
In still, dark nights (you are asleep),
And hold his hands, and try to weep.

I cannot weep; I cannot pray —
Why grow so pale, and turn away?
Do you expect to hold me fast
By pretty legends in the past?

It is a woman's province, then,
To be content with what has been?
To wear the wreath of withered flowers,

That crowned her in the bridal hours?

Still, I am yours: this idle strife
Stirs but the surface of my life:
And if you would but ask once more,
"How goes the heart?" or at the door

Imploring stand, and knock again,
I might forget this sense of pain,
And down oblivion's sullen stream
Would float the memory of my dream!

NAMELESS PAIN.

I should be happy with my lot:
A wife and mother — is it not
Enough for me to be content?
What other blessing could be sent?

A quiet house, and homely ways,
That make each day like other days;
I only see Time's shadow now
Darken the hair on baby's brow!

No world's work ever comes to me,
No beggar brings his misery;
I have no power, no healing art
With bruisèd soul or broken heart.

I read the poets of the age,
'Tis lotus-eating in a cage;
I study Art, but Art is dead
To one who clamors to be fed

With milk from Nature's rugged breast,
Who longs for Labor's lusty rest.

O foolish wish! I still should pine
If any other lot were mine.

A BABY SONG.

Come, white angels, to baby and me;
Touch his blue eyes with the image of sleep,
In his surprise he will cease to weep;
Hush, child, the angels are coming to thee!

Come, white doves, to baby and me;
Softly whirr in the silent air,
Flutter about his golden hair:
Hark, child, the doves are cooing to thee!

Come, white lilies, to baby and me;
Drowsily nod before his eyes,
So full of wonder, so round and wise:
Hist, child, the lily-bells tinkle for thee!

Come, white moon, to baby and me;
Gently glide o'er the ocean of sleep,
Silver the waves of its shadowy deep:
Sleep, child, and the whitest of dreams to thee.

THE WIFE SPEAKS.

Husband, to-day could you and I behold
The sun that brought us to our bridal morn
Rising so splendid in the winter sky
(We thought fair spring returned), when we were wed;
Could the shades vanish from these fifteen years,
Which stand like columns guarding the approach

To that great temple of the double soul
That is as one—would you turn back, my dear,
And, for the sake of Love's mysterious dream,
As old as Adam and as sweet as Eve,
Take me, as I took you, and once more go
Towards that goal which none of us have reached?
Contesting battles which but prove a loss,
The victor vanquished by the wounded one;
Teaching each other sacrifice of self,
True immolation to the marriage bond;
Learning the joys of birth, the woe of death,
Leaving in chaos all the hopes of life—
Heart-broken, yet with courage pressing on
For fame and fortune, artists needing both?
Or, would you rather—I will acquiesce—
Since we must choose what is, and are grown gray,
Stay in life's desert, watch our setting sun,
Calm as those statues in Egyptian sands,
Hand clasping hand, with patience and with peace,
Wait for a future which contains no past?

THE HUSBAND SPEAKS.

Dearest, though I have sung a many songs,
Yet have I never sung one from my heart,
Save to thee only—and such private songs
Are as the silent, secret kiss of Love!
My heart, I say, so sacred was, and is,
I kept, I keep it, from all eyes but thine,
Because it is no longer mine, but thine,
Given thee forever, when I gave myself
That winter morning—was it years ago?
To me it seems the dream of yesterday!
You have not lost the face I married then,
Albeit a trifle paler—not to-night—
Nor I the eyes that saw then, and see still,

What every man should see in her he weds!
I wander ... wisely, let me, since my words
Conceal what none but you and I should know, —
The love I bear you, who have been, and are
Strong in the strength and weakness of your sex —
Queen of my household, mistress of my heart,
My children's mother, and my always friend;
In one word, Sweet, sweetest of all words — Wife!

"ONE MORN I LEFT HIM IN HIS BED."

One morn I left him in his bed;
A moment after some one said,
"Your child is dying — he is dead."

We made him ready for his rest,
Flowers in his hair, and on his breast
His little hands together prest.

We sailed by night across the sea;
So, floating from the world were we,
Apart from sympathy, we Three.

The wild sea moaned, the black clouds spread
Moving shadows on its bed,
But one of us lay midship dead.

I saw his coffin sliding down
The yellow sand in yonder town,
Where I put on my sorrow's crown.

And we returned; in this drear place
Never to see him face to face,
I thrust aside the living race.

Mothers, who mourn with me to-day,

Oh, understand me, when I say,
I cannot weep, I cannot pray;

I gaze upon a hidden store,
His books, his toys, the clothes he wore,
And cry, "Once more, to me, *once* more!"

Then take, from me, this simple verse,
That you may know what I rehearse—
A grief—your and my Universe!

BEFORE THE MIRROR.

Now like the Lady of Shalott,
I dwell within an empty room,
And through the day and through the night
I sit before an ancient loom.

And like the Lady of Shalott
I look into a mirror wide,
Where shadows come, and shadows go,
And ply my shuttle as they glide.

Not as she wove the yellow wool,
Ulysses' wife, Penelope;
By day a queen among her maids,
But in the night a woman, she,

Who, creeping from her lonely couch,
Unraveled all the slender wool;
Or, with a torch, she climbed the towers,
To fire the fagots on the roof!

But weaving with a steady hand
The shadows, whether false or true,
I put aside a doubt which asks

"Among these phantoms what are you?"

For not with altar, tomb, or urn,
Or long-haired Greek with hollow shield,
Or dark-prowed ship with banks of oars,
Or banquet in the tented field;

Or Norman knight in armor clad,
Waiting a foe where four roads meet;
Or hawk and hound in bosky dell,
Where dame and page in secret greet;

Or rose and lily, bud and flower,
My web is broidered. Nothing bright
Is woven here: the shadows grow
Still darker in the mirror's light!

And as my web grows darker too,
Accursed seems this empty room;
For still I must forever weave
These phantoms by this ancient loom.

"THE SHADOWS ON THE WATER REACH."

The shadows on the water reach
My shadow on the beach;
I see the dark trees on the shore,
The fisher's oar.

I met her by the sea last night,
A little maid in white;
I shall never meet her more
On the shore.

Ho! fisher, hoist your idle sail,
And whistle for a gale;

My ship is waiting in the bay,
Row away!

A SUMMER NIGHT.

I feel the breath of the summer night,
Aromatic fire:
The trees, the vines, the flowers are astir
With tender desire.

The white moths flutter about the lamp,
Enamoured with light;
And a thousand creatures softly sing
A song to the night!

But I am alone, and how can I sing
Praises to thee?
Come, Night! unveil the beautiful soul
That waiteth for me.

"FAN ME WITH THESE LILIES FAIR."

Fan me with these lilies fair,
Twine their stems around your arm:
Put your feet upon these roses,
Then you'll please me to a charm.

Charm me with your violet eyes,
Kneel, and with your sweet lips meet
The flaming buds of mine, athirst
In the roses at your feet!

"Leave the lilies on the lake,

Do not break its pale repose:
Tear your heart with cruel thorns,
Such as grow beneath the rose.

"So you love me? You are mine?
Break from yon dead tree a bough,
Lay it down among these roses—
Ah! I do not charm you now!"

"OH, THE WILD, WILD DAYS OF YOUTH!"

Oh, the wild, wild days of youth!
My royal youth;
My blood was then my king:
Maybe a little mad,
But full of truth!

Oh, my lips were like a rose!
And my heart, too;
It was torn out leaf by leaf:
Ah! there be none that know
How the leaves flew!

Oh, they dropped in the wine!
The royal wine;
There were showers for the girls,
Crowns for their white brows,
And for mine!

"ON MY BED OF A WINTER NIGHT."

On my bed of a winter night,
Deep in a sleep and deep in a dream,

What care I for the wild wind's scream,
What to me is its crooked flight?

On the sea of a summer day,
Wrapped in the folds of a snowy sail,
What care I for the fitful gale,
Now in earnest, now in play?

What care I for the fitful wind,
That groans in a gorge, or sighs in a tree?
Groaning and sighing are nothing to me,
For I am a man of steadfast mind.

"HALLO! MY FANCY, WHITHER WILT THOU GO?"

Swift as the tide in the river
The blood flows through my heart,
At the curious little fancy
That to-morrow we must part.

It seems to me all over,
The last words have been said;
And I have the curious fancy
To-morrow will find me dead!

YOU LEFT ME.

You left me, and the anguish passed,
And passed the day, and passed the night—
A blank in which my senses failed;
Then slowly came an inward light.

So plain it reproduced the hours

We lived as one,—the books we read,
Our quiet walks and pleasant talks—
Love, by your spirit was I led?

Oh, love, the vision grows too dear,
I live in visions—I pursue
Them only; come, your rival meet,
My future bring, it will be—*you!*

"O FRIEND, BEGIN A LOFTIER SONG."

O friend, begin a loftier song.
Confusion falls upon your mind;
A sense of evil makes you blind;
"What use," you say, "is it to be?
I know not GOD, GOD knows not me!"

O friend, begin a loftier song.
In other minds you place no trust:
You tread your laurels in the dust:
You see no Future, Hope has fled,
Youth had its dreams, but Youth is dead.

O friend, begin a loftier song.
"The sweet ideal of past years
Speaks in my songs, they are my tears:
I'll weep no more, I'll sing no lays
To bury Youth for idle praise!"

O friend, begin a loftier song.
Come through the gateway of the Past,
Dear friend. The world will hear at last
The little songs the poets sing:
Do thou with anthems make it ring!

"NOW THAT THE PAIN IS GONE, I TOO CAN SMILE."

Now that the pain is gone, I too can smile
At such a foolish picture; you and me
Together in that moonlit summer night,
Within the shadow of an aspen-tree.

My hand was on your shoulder: I grew wild:
The blood seethed furiously through my heart!
But you—Oh, you were saintly calm, and cold;
You moved my hand, and said, "'T is best we part!"

My face fell on the bands of your fair hair,
A moonbeam struck across my hungry eye,
And struck across your balmy crimson mouth:
I longed to kiss you, and I longed to die!

Die in the shadow of the trembling tree,
Trembling my soul away upon your breast.
You smiled, and drifted both your snowy hands
Against my forehead, and your fingers pressed

Faintly and slow adown my burning face;
A keen sense of the woman touched you then,
The nice dramatic sense you women have,
Playing upon the feelings of us men!

Long years have passed since that midsummer night,
But still I feel the creeping of your hand
Along my face. If I return once more,
And in the shadow of that tree should stand

With you there—Answer! Would you kiss me back?
Would you reject me if I sued again?—
How strange this is! I think my madness lasts,
Although I'm sure I have forgot the pain!

THE COLONEL'S SHIELD.

Your picture, slung about my neck
The day we went afield,
Swung out before the trench;
It caught the eye of rank and file,
Who knew "The Colonel's Shield."

I thrust it back, and with my men
(Our General rode ahead)
We stormed the great redoubt,
As if it were an easy thing,
But rows of us fell dead!

Your picture hanging on my neck,
Up with my men I rushed;
We made an awful charge:
And then my horse, "The Lady Bess,"
Dropped, and—my leg was crushed!

The blood of battle in my veins
(A blue-coat dragged me out),—
But I remembered you;
I kissed your picture—did you know?
And yelled, "For the redoubt!"

The Twenty-fourth, my scarred old dogs,
Growled back, "He'll put us through;
We'll take him in our arms:
Our picture there—the girl he loves,
Shall see what we can do."

The foe was silenced—so were we.
I lay upon the field,
Among the Twenty-fourth;
Your picture, shattered on my breast,

Had proved "The Colonel's Shield."

A FEW IDLE WORDS.

So, I must believe that I loved you once!
These letters say so;
And here is your picture—how you have changed!
It was long ago.

The gloss is worn from this lock of black hair—
You can have them all,
And with these treasures a few idle words,
That I will not recall.

What a child I was when you met me first!
Was I handsome then?
I think you remember the very night,
It was half-past ten,

When you came upstairs, so tired of the men,
And tired of the wine;
You said you loved lilies (my dress was white),
And hated to dine.

The dowagers nodded behind their fans;
I played an old song;
You told an old tale, I thought it so new,
And I thought so long.

True, I had read the "Arabian Nights,"
And "Amadis de Gaul;"
But I never had found a modern knight
In our books at the Hall.

You tore your hand with the thorns of the rose
That looped up my sleeve,

And a drop of red blood fell on my arm —
You asked, "Do you grieve?"

That drop of your blood made mine flow fast;
But you sipped your tea
With a nonchalant air, and balanced the spoon,
And balanced poor me,

In the scale with my stocks, and farms, and mines.
Did it tremble at all?
When my cousin, the heir, turned up one day,
We both had a fall!

Well, we meet again, and I look at you
With a quiet surprise;
I think your ennui possesses me now,
And am quite as wise.

To me it was only a dream of love,
A defeat to you:
It was not your first, may be not your last —
Here, take them — Adieu!

VERS DE SOCIÉTÉ.

This chain of white arms round the room —
The demon waltz — bewilders me:
Or am I drunk with this good wine?
Vive la compagnie!

"My friend, young Highboys, have you met?"
"O yes: how do? good brandy here!"
The wretch's mother, in her youth,
Was famous for her beer!

Before his patent scraper sold

Old Highboys used to beat them all!
See what Society has done—
He's holding her cashmere shawl!

How is it, Madam, that I know
The guests at once? Wipe off the paint—
Convention daubs us all alike,
Sinner as well as Saint!

I see you in the crimson chair,
Behind your jewelled Spanish fan,
Slipping your bracelets up and down,
Flashing your eyes on the man

Who plays the harp; he twangs an air
You understand—you've met before;
How many lessons did you take?
Madam, you need no more.

Tiger of fifty! So you've bought
This pretty girl in the Honiton lace.
Now she's abroad, she quite forgets
She shudders in your embrace.

Dowagers, stiff in black brocades,
Worry the waiters—sweep their trays:
How they scowl at the foolish men
Basking in Beauty's blaze!

Saunters a poet, munching cake:
"Very distinguished." "Did you buy
Your lace at Beck's?" "Why, how he laughs!"
"But his verses make one cry!"

Idle poet, a word with you:
You sing too much of love's sweet wrong,
Of rosy cheeks, and purple wine:
Give us a loftier song.

The coachmen stamp upon the steps;
Our hostess looks towards the door;
Our host twists round his limp cravat,
Pronouncing the thing a bore!

Our skeletons will be stirring soon;
Something already touches me:
Off, till I drain one bottle more!
Vive la compagnie!

THE RACE.

The guests were gathered in the ancient park
Of my Lord Wynne, and he was now their mark
For wit and gossip—quite the usual way,
Where one bestows, and no one need repay.
"A stumbling-block his pride; his heart's in strife
Between two women, which to choose for wife.
He's always hovering round that lovely girl,
His lawyer's daughter, who will never furl
Her flag of pride: she rivals Gilbert there.
Now watch their meeting; none more bravely wear
Their beauty, recognize a woman's own,
Than Clara Mercome. Gilbert Wynne has sown
His wild oats for her sake; yet he delays,
And with my Lady Bond divides his days.
Who bets on beauty, hedges in on age;
Which tries the flight to perch in Lord Wynne's cage?
Will Lady Bond or Clara be the queen?
For Lady Bond is certain of her lien."
He heard this talk while standing by a beech—
Hugh Wynne—and planned how he might overreach
Gilbert and Clara, break the pride of both,
Part them for good, or make them plight their troth.
"Now for a race," he cried, "to Martin's Mill;
The boats are here; behold, the lake is still.

Here, Gilbert, take your oar; I'll follow soon,
Though sunset's nigh—to-night is harvest-moon.
Let go the rope, the knot's inside; take these,
Arrange a seat, adjust it at your ease.
She's here. Miss Mercome, you will help him win
The race, and will not count my wager sin."
And he was gone; the pair were face to face.
"I'll take the oars," he gasped; "we'll win this race."
He never felt his heart so in his breast.
"I hope you will forgive my cousin's jest?"
A haughty murmur was her sole reply.
No rowers followed. Never did swallows fly
So swift, or dip the lake like Gilbert's oars.
He was watchful, careless she. "There soars
A heron, quite a feature of your state:
Are gems and peacocks, tell me, still in date?
How deep the woods upon the water steal,
One to the other making soft appeal!"
"Not being human, wood and water meet
In their own speech, and soulless things are sweet
Together. So they are to me. I like
To watch the herons by the sedgy dike;
They keep me tranquil; and I love to feed
The pike in yon old pool; they help to lead—
Why, here is Martin's Bridge, and yet no boats!
Shall we return?" Said Clara then, "There floats
A lily bed beyond; let's shoot beneath
The bridge, and lilies pull; I want a wreath."
He knew the channel narrow; it was dark;
But his heart leaped at this relenting mark.
He drew his oars up, pointed in the helm,
And shot in the cool gloom. He thought no realm
On which the sun had shone was half so bright.
And somehow Clara thought it nice as light.
The waters swirled so swift that in the noise
Clara grew dizzy; Gilbert lost his poise,
And lost an oar; with a confusing shock
The boat was grinding—stopped against a rock.
"Gilbert, my dear, are we not going down?"

"Dearest, my love, we were not born to drown.
Oh, kiss me; we are safe; and grant me now
Yourself. I'll gather lilies for your brow;
And Hugh will know that I have won the race,
And Clara, my dear wife, her rightful place."

THE WOLF-TAMER.

Through the gorge of snow we go,
Tracking, tramping soft and slow,
With our paws and sheathèd claws,
So we swing along the snow,
Crowding, crouching to your pipes —
Shining serpents! Well you know,
When your lips shall cease to blow
Airs that lure us through the snow,
We shall fall upon your race
Who do wear a different face.
Who were spared in yonder vale?
Not a man to tell the tale!
Blow, blow, serpent pipes,
Slow we follow: — all our troop —
Every wolf of wooded France,
Down from all the Pyrenees —
Shall they follow, follow you,
In your dreadful music-trance?
Mark it by our tramping paws,
Hidden fangs, and sheathèd claws?
You have seen the robber bands
Tear men's tongues and cut their hands,
For ransom — we ask none — begone,
For the tramping of our paws,
Marking all your music's laws,
Numbs the lust of ear and eye;
Or — let us go beneath the snow,
And silent die — as wolves should die!

THE ABBOT OF UNREASON.

I looked over the balustrade—
The twilight had come—
And saw the pretty waiting-maid
Kiss Roland, the page.

My lady heard the wolf-dog's chain
Clank on the floor;
Sly Roland caught it up again,
And whistled a song.

Oh! they think that my heart is cold,
Under my gown;
Not till I blacken into mould
Will it cease to burn.

Burn, burn for such sweet red lips!
I am almost mad,
Even to touch her finger tips,
When we meet alone.

Roland, the page, goes here and there,
Loving, and loved,
Women like his devil-may-care,
Till they are forgot!

Whether I am in castle or inn,
With sinner or saint,
Never can I a woman win,—
I am but a priest!

EL MANOLO.

In the still, dark shade of the palace wall,
Where the peacocks strut,
Where the queen may have heard my madrigal,
Together we sat.

My sombrero hid the fire in my eyes,
And shaded her own:
This serge cloak stifled her sweet little cries,
When I kissed her mouth!

The pale olive trees on the distant plain,
The jagged blue rocks,
The vaporous sea-like mountain chain,
Dropped into the night.

We saw the lights in the palace flare;
The musicians played:
The red guards slashed and sabred the stair,
And cursed the old king.

In the long black shade of the palace wall,
We sat the night through;
Under my cloak—but I cannot tell all—
The queen may have seen!

MERCEDES.

Under a sultry, yellow sky,
On the yellow sand I lie;
The crinkled vapors smite my brain,
I smoulder in a fiery pain.

Above the crags the condor flies;
He knows where the red gold lies,

He knows where the diamonds shine;—
If I knew, would she be mine?

Mercedes in her hammock swings;
In her court a palm-tree flings
Its slender shadow on the ground,
The fountain falls with silver sound.

Her lips are like this cactus cup;
With my hand I crush it up;
I tear its flaming leaves apart;—
Would that I could tear her heart!

Last night a man was at her gate;
In the hedge I lay in wait;
I saw Mercedes meet him there,
By the fireflies in her hair.

I waited till the break of day,
Then I rose and stole away;
But left my dagger in the gate;—
Now she knows her lover's fate!

THE BULL-FIGHT.

Eleven o'clock:
Here are our cups of chocolate.
Montez will fight the bulls to-day—
All Madrid knows that:
Queen Christina is going in state:
Dolores will go with her little fan!

Lace up my shoe;
Put on my Basquina;
Can you see my black eyes?
I am Manuel's duchess.

In front of the box of the Queen and the Duke
Dolores sits, flirting her fan;
The church of St. Agnes stands on the right,
And its shadow falls on the picadors;
On their lean steeds they prance in the ring,
Hidalgo-fashion, their hands on their hips.

"Ha! Toro! Toro!"
Hoh! the horses are gored;
Now for the men.
"Ha! Toro! Toro!"
Every man over the barrier!

Not so; for there the bull-fighter stands;
Some little applause from the royal box,
And *"Montez! Montez!"* from a thousand throats!

The bull bows fine, though snorting with rage,
His fore-leg makes little holes in the ground;
But Montez stands still; his ribbons don't flutter!
Saints, what a leap!
His rosette is on the bull's black horn;
Montez is pale; but his great eye shines
When Dolores cries — *"Kisses for Montez!"*
Fie! Manuel's duchess!

A minute longer the fight is done,
The mule-bells tinkle, the bull rides off;
Montez twirls a new diamond ring,
And Dolores goes home for chocolate.

ON THE CAMPAGNA.

Stop on the Appian Way,
In the Roman Campagna;

Stop at my tomb,
The tomb of Cecilia Metella.
To-day as you see it,
Alaric saw it, ages ago,
When he, with his pale-visaged Goths,
Sat at the gates of Rome,
Reading his Runic shield.
Odin, thy curse remains!

Beneath these battlements
My bones were stirred with Roman pride,
Though centuries before my Romans died
Now my bones are dust; the Goths are dust.
The river-bed is dry where sleeps the king,
My tomb remains!

When Rome commanded the earth
Great were the Metelli:
I was Metella's wife;
I loved him — and I died.
Then with slow patience built he this memorial:
Each century marks his love.

Pass by on the Appian Way
The tomb of Cecilia Metella;
Wild shepherds alone seek its shelter,
Wild buffaloes tramp at its base.
Deep is its desolation,
Deep as the shadow of Rome!

THE QUEEN DEPOSED.

I was the queen of Karl, a northern king:
Amazon Olga, and I rode his Ban,
A stallion in the royal ring
Who would not bear a man.

And in Ban's saddle did I feel the pains
For my first-born, the king's sole hope, his heir;
My Karl himself would loose the reins,
Would take me up the stair.

Low was the murmur of the royal troops
Below, I saw the tapers' twinkling light;
I heard a cry — "My queen, she droops!"
Then fell eternal night.

No more was Olga queen for any king;
The pathway round a throne she could not tread,
Nor triumph in the royal ring —
The boy she bore was dead!

The cloister hers; she chose the cloak and hood,
And beads of olive-wood, a pouch for alms;
So begged she, Christ, for thy dear rood,
Laus Deo sang thy psalms!

Why am I here? This country is my king's;
The lovely river, wooded hills above;
Old St. Sebastian's church-bell rings —
There flies the silver dove

That flitted by the day we came to praise
Our gracious Mary for a granted prayer;
Heralds, trumps, the same gay maze
Of troops — King Karl is there!

Laus Deo with a child, and with his mate —
She wins the throne by bringing him a son:
Babes make or mar our queenly fate —
My woman's life is done.

A UNIT.

When I was camping on the Volga's banks,
The trader Zanthon with a leash of mares
Went by my tent. I knew the wily Jew,
And he knew me. He muttered as he passed,
"The last Bathony, and his tusks are grown.
A broken 'scutcheon is a 'scutcheon still,
And Amine's token in my caftan lies, —
Amine, who weeps and wails for his return."
He caught my eye, and slipped inside the tent.
"Haw, Zanthon, up from Poland, at your tricks!
How veer the boars on old Bathony's towers?
True to the winds that blow on Poland's plains?"
"They bite the dust, my lord, as beast to beast.
When Poles conspire, conspiracy alone
Survives to hover in the murky air.
My lord, Bathony's gates are left ajar
For you to enter, or — remain outside;
The forest holds the secret you surprised,
And men are there, to dare as they have dared."
"Haw, Zanthon, tell me of the palatine.
The air of Russia makes a man forget
He was a man elsewhere: the trumpets' squeal
I follow, and the thud of drums. You spoke
As if I were of princely birth: hark ye,
Battalion is the call I listen to."
"My lord, the cranes that plunder in your fens,
The doves that nest within your woods I saw
Fly round the gaping walls, and plume their wings
Upon your father's grave. Do you know this?"
"A token, Zanthon? so — a withered flower!
You think I wore one in my sword-hilt once?
Methinks there is no perfume in this flower.
Watch, while I fling it on the Volga's tide.
The chief, my father, sent me with a curse
To travel in the steppes, and so I do.
The air of Russia makes a man forget
He was a man elsewhere, for love or hope,

And as he marches, he becomes but this.
Haw, Zanthon, would you learn the reason why?
Search on the Caucasus, the northern seas,
Look in the sky or over earth, then ask,
The answer everywhere will be, *The Tzar.*"

ZANTHON—MY FRIEND.

I, knight-at-arms, in my own forest lost!
Count of the empire, heir to crags and caves,
And brother to the eagle and the fox!
The music of the thunder, and the wind
Among the arches of the oaks, may choir
A requiem for my passing soul. But hist!
A footstep in the leaves—some poaching hind
Or gypsy trapping game—Holà! holà!
Perhaps the kobolds are abroad to-night.
Zanthon knows well these mountain-folk entice.
The woods divide, dawn breaks, I see the verge;
Bathony's stronghold on the Polish plains
Should top the wilderness: were Zanthon here,
To boast his prowess in our hunting bouts,
I would not cuff nor flout him, could we sight
In the old way, with fanfaron, the boars
On the old battlements, our ancient badge.
That lie to Zanthon on the Volga's banks,
When Amine sent the wild rose by his hand,
Was Satan's wile. I played the Cossack well.
With shame my mustache bristled when I said,
"Troopers must forage where the grain is grown:
I share my kopecks with the village priest,
Who winnows peccadillos by the sheaf."
Then Zanthon, laughing in his foxy beard:
"When Amine meets me in the plane-tree walk
(Where pairing little finches seek to build,
We saw the cuckoo thieve their nests when boys),

Shall I then tell her, in my peasant way,
Your broken promise, and her troth denied?"
And he was gone — gone, with the stud he bought
From Schamyl's son, up by Caucasus way,
Leaving me solitude to reason with.
Around me, then, an odor swept — the rose!
It plagued my nostrils day and night, in gusts
It blew, but one way only — towards Amine.
At cards it smote me, in the saddle puffed,
Through my tent walls at night its withered blast
Pierced, and changed me in my wavering dreams.
What spell was this, by love or friendship sent?
Across the steppes I followed Zanthon, close, —
He might have heard the whinny of my mare;
Verst after verst, the measure of her hoofs
Beat out a rhythm, like a cackling laugh.
But on the frontier my poor Sesma fell:
I heard the ravens croaking from the hills.
The sun has burned away the valley's mist.
And in the silent, tranquil morning air
A mirage rises of my ruined walls:
Gold-colored, crystal-edged, the banners flash.
The rooks are stringing for the old beech copse.
This gully crossed, the bridge that spans the stream —
But halte-lâ, my heart crowds up my breast,
For this is Poland, Mother of my Soul!
Quoth Zanthon, watching in the plane-tree walk,
"My fine Bathony comes to join the feast,
And raise the conopeum for my bride.
I pay the kopecks to the priest to-day,
But Amine in his sheaf will not be bound."

ACHILLES IN ORCUS.

From thy translucent waves, great Thetis, rise!
Mother divine, hear, and take back the gift

Thou gavest me of valor and renown,
And then seek Zeus, but not with loosened zone
For dalliance; entreat him to restore
Me, Achilles, to the earth, to the black earth,
The nourisher of men, not these pale shades,
Whose shapes have learned the presage of thy doom;
They flit between me and the wind-swept plain
Of Troy, the banners over Ilion's walls,
The zenith of my prowess, and my fate.
Give me again the breath of life, not death.
Would I could tarry in the timbered tent,
As when I wept Patroclus, when, by night,
Old Priam crept, kissing my knees with tears
For Hector's corse, the hero I laid low.
My panoply was like the gleam of fire
When in the dust I dragged him at my wheels,
My heart was iron,—he despoiled my friend.
Cast on these borders of eternal gloom,
Now comes Odysseus with his wandering crew;
He pours libations in the deep-dug trench,
While airy forms in multitudes press near,
And listen to the echoes of my praise.
His consolation vain, he hails me, "Prince!"
Vain is his speech: "No man before thy time,
Achilles, lived more honored; here thou art
Supreme, the ruler in these dread abodes."
Speak not so easily to me of death,
Great Odysseus! Rather would I be
The meanest hind, and bring the bleating lambs
From down the grassy hills, or with a goad
To prod the hungry swine in beechen woods,
Than over the departed to bear sway.
Then from the clouds to note the warning cry
Of the harsh crane; to see the Pleiads rise,
The vine and fig-tree shoot, the olive bud;
To hear the chirping swallows in the dawn,
The thieving cuckoo laughing in the leaves!
So, may Achilles pass his palace gate,
And later heroes strike Achilles' lyre!

ABOVE THE TREE.

Why should I tarry here, to be but one
To eke out doubt, and suffer with the rest?
Why should I labor to become a name,
And vaunt, as did Ulysses to his mates,
"I am a part of all that I have met."
A wily seeker to suffice myself!
As when the oak's young leaves push off the old,
So from this tree of life man drops away,
And all the boughs are peopled quick by spring
Above the furrows of forgotten graves.
The one we thought had made the nation's creed,
Whose death would rive us like a thunderbolt,
Dropped down—a sudden rustling in the leaves,
A knowledge of the gap, and that was all!
The robin flitting on his frozen mound
Is more than he. Whoever dies, gives up
Unfinished work, which others, tempted, claim
And carry on. I would go free, and change
Into a star above the multitude,
To shine afar, and penetrate where those
Who in the darkling boughs are prisoned close,
But when they catch my rays, will borrow light,
Believing it their own, and it will serve.

TO AN ARTIST.

To me, long absent from the world of art,
You bring the clouded mountains, my desire,
The tranquil river, and the stormy sea,
The far, pale morning, and the crimson eve,

And silent days, that brood among lush leaves,
When, in the afternoon, the summer sun
Is gliding down the hazy yellow west,
And my soul's atmosphere rests in the scene,
Until I dream the boundaries of my life
May hold an unknown, coming happiness.
How shall I, then, to show my gratitude,
But offer you a picture drawn in words—
With all the art I have,—in black and white!

A LANDSCAPE.

Between me and the woods along the bay
The swallows circle through the darkling mist,
The robins breast the grass, and they divide
This solitude with me. The rippling sea
And sunset clouds, the sea gulls' flashing flight
From looming isles beyond—I watch them now
With a new sense. Where are the swallows' young,
And where the robins' nests? Year after year
They hover round this ancient house, and I,
Within as heedless, saw the long years pass,
Nor ever dreamed a day like this might come—
A day when mourners go about the street
For one who always loved his fellow-men.
The windflower trembles in the woods, the sod
Is full of violets, the orchards rain
Their scented blossoms. May unfolds its leaves—
Nature's eternal mystery to renew.
Must man be less than leaf or flower, and end?
If I go hence, when this departed soul
Has left no human tie to bind me now,
When spring unfolds, and I recall his past,
Will their remembrance lead me here again,
To teach me that his spirit comes to show
That Nature is eternal for man's sake?

FROM THE HEADLAND.

I hear the waters of some inlet now
Come lapping to the fringe of yonder wood,
The storm-bent firs, and oaks along the cliff.
The yellow leaves are glistening in the grass,
The grassy slope I climb this autumn day.
Ensnaring me, the brambles clutch my feet,
As if constraining me to be a guest
To the wild, silent populace they shield.
It cannot say, nor I, why we are here.
What is my recompense upon this soil,
For other paths are mine if I go hence,
Still must I make the mystery my quest?
For here or there, I think, one sways my will.
There is no show of beauty to delight
The vision here, or strike the electric chord
Which makes the present and the past as one.
No thickets where the thrushes sing in maze
Of green, no silver-threaded waterfalls
In vales, where summer sleeps in darkling woods
With sunlit glades, and pools where lilies blow.
Here, but the wiry grass and sorrel beds,
The gaping edges of the sand ravines,
Whose shifting sides are tufted with dull herbs,
Drooping above a brook, that sluggish creeps
Down to the whispering rushes in the marsh.
And this is all, until I reach the cliff,
And on the headland's verge I stand, enthralled
Before the gulf of the unquenchable sea —
The sea, inexorable in its might,
Circling the pebbly beach with limpid tides,
Storming in bays whose margins fade in mist;
Now blue and silent as a noonday sky,
At twilight now the pearly rollers shake

The sunset's trail of violet and gold;
Or black, when rushing on the rocky isles
Anchored in waves that bellow to the winds.
I watch till comes the night; the moonlight falls,
The silvery deep on some far journey goes,
To solve for me, I think, this mystery.

AS ONE.

When I, enclosed within the city's walls,
Behold the multitudes that come and go,
Hands clenched on gain, and nature all denied,
Then I recall, recall the drift of time.

But when she proffered all her wealth to me,
The first faint blossom of the spring I share,
The latest autumn leaf, the last green blade,
Then I forget, forget the drift of time.

The months go by, and take me in their train,
The vesture wrapping them enfolds me too,
And all the journey through we seem as one,
And I forget, forget the drift of time.

I hear the bluebird's call in windy dawns,
The robin's cheery note from dewy fields,
The swallow's cry along the pool at eve,
And I forget, forget the drift of time.

When hedges give the prophecy of birds,
And sunbeams play on the expectant boughs,
The leaves uncurl and fill their veins with life,
And I forget, forget the drift of time.

I watch a tumult in the summer skies,
A blur of sunshine, and the rush of rain,

The tempest dying in the twilight's hush,
And I forget, forget the drift of time.

When winter woods are armored by the frost,
And all the highways filled with soundless snows,
Then comes the sun to show his golden palm,
And I forget, forget the drift of time.

The mountains look upon me and the sea —
I hover on their crests in silver mists,
And with the waters pass beyond their verge,
And I forget, forget the drift of time.

THE VISITINGS OF TRUTH KNOWN ELSEWHERE.

Spending abroad these varied autumn days,
Their melancholy legend I deny.
They keep a vanished treasure I will seek,
And follow on a track of mystic hopes.
While watching in thy atmosphere, I see
The form of beauty changes, not its soul.
When with the Spring, the flying feet of youth
Spurning the present as it passed, and me,
I thought the world a mere environment
To hold my wishes and my happiness.
I have forgot that foolish, vain belief,
Now in my sere and yellow leaf, serene,
I offer Autumn all my homage now.
The eddies, whirling, rustling in my path,
Lure me like sprites, and from the leaves a voice:
"Say not our lesson is decay; we fall,
And lo, the naked trees in beauty lift
Their delicate tracery against the sky.
On the pale verdure of the grass we spread
A shining web of scarlet, bronze, and gold;
When the rain comes, the oaks uphold us still.

The holly shines, and waits the Christmas chimes,
Beneath the branches of the evergreens."
November's clouds without a shadow lift
The purple mountains of its airy sphere,
And all my purpose waits upon them now.
Day fades—a rose above the darkling sea,
And from the amber sky clear twilight falls;
The orange woods grow black, and I go forth,
And as I go, the noiseless airs pass by,
And touch me like the petals of a flower;
The cricket chirps me in the warm, dry sod,
Drowsy, and I would pipe a cheery strain;
But from the pines I hear the call of night,
And round the quiet earth the stars wheel up,
With me eternal, and I stay beneath,
Until I fade into the fading plain.

WE MUST WAIT.

The testimony of my loss and gain
Will I give utterance to, though none may hear.
When long ago, bereft of all I loved,
I sought in Nature recompense, implored
For pity, solace, or forgetfulness,
"The dear, familiar seasons as they pass,
The seal of memory on every place,"
I said, "will give the sympathy I seek,
The restoration which they owe to me."
By day and night I prayed as futile prayers
As the wind's shriek in lonesome winter nights;
By the sea they fell as empty as the shells
Upon its sands, uncertain as its mists.
With them I tracked the shadows of the woods,
And sowed them in the fields among the seed;
Whoso reaped harvest, I could gather none.
I wandered in the thickets, giving tongue

Like a lost hound, dazed by their solitude,
The while birds called their mates, the lilies blazed,
And roses opened to the wandering airs.
They vanished with the leaves that voyaged the brook,
Which babbled of no story but its own.
How blind I was to Nature's liberty!
Grief stalked beside me, I was sore beset,
And could not hear the turning of Time's wheel.
Still were the skies serene, the earth most fair,
When with the doleful chant of dust to dust
Mingled the laughter of this sunlit sea;
And through my tears I saw the ripples dance,
And June's sweet breezes kiss the swaying elms.
As he who turns the key within his door
And gazes at his walls before he goes,
Then forward sets his steps — so I set mine
To join a band whose purpose was to find
A world of action; but my heart was cold,
My mind supine. Yet I remained with them,
And answered to the roll called Honor, Fame!
Where were my memories and my ardent prayers?
The years stood far behind, their columns graved
Deep with the adage which youth names *No More*.
Like one who enters some old storied hall,
And down its vista suddenly beholds
A banner waving out its old device
Of victory — so suddenly I felt
My later life a void. I was recalled!
My prayers were answered, and behold me here;
Within the pale of all my loss and gain,
The dear, familiar seasons as they pass,
The seal of memory on every place,
Bestow the restoration which I sought.
At peace, I know, as those who suffer know,
There is no secret we can wrest at will
From Nature. Time must bring and share with her
The gift of resignation, cure for grief,
And cast upon our ways this ray of hope —
That I, the lost, and Nature may be one.

UNRETURNING.

Now all the flowers that ornament the grass,
Wherever meadows are and placid brooks,
Must fall—the "glory of the grass" must fall.
Year after year I see them sprout and spread—
The golden, glossy, tossing buttercups,
The tall, straight daisies and red clover globes,
The swinging bellwort and the blue-eyed bent,
With nameless plants as perfect in their hues—
Perfect in root and branch, their plan of life,
As if the intention of a soul were there:
I see them flourish as I see them fall!
But he, who once was growing with the grass,
And blooming with the flowers, my little son,
Fell, withered—dead, nor has revived again!
Perfect and lovely, needful to my sight,
Why comes he not to ornament my days?
The barren fields forget their barrenness,
The soulless earth mates with these soulless things,
Why should I not obtain *my* recompense?
The budding spring should bring, or summer's prime,
At least a vision of the vanished child,
And let his heart commune with mine again,
Though in a dream—his life was but a dream;
Then might I wait with patient cheerfulness,
That cheerfulness which keeps one's tears unshed,
And blinds the eyes with pain—the passage slow
Of other seasons, and be still and cold
As the earth is when shrouded in the snow,
Or passive, like it, when the boughs are stripped
In autumn, and the leaves roll everywhere.
And he should go again; for winter's snows,
And autumn's melancholy voice, in winds,
In waters, and in woods, belong to me,

To me—a faded soul; for, as I said,
The sense of all his beauty, sweetness, comes
When blossoms are the sweetest; when the sea,
Sparkling and blue, cries to the sun in joy,
Or, silent, pale, and misty waits the night,
Till the moon, pushing through the veiling cloud,
Hangs naked in its heaving solitude:
When feathery pines wave up and down the shore,
And the vast deep above holds gentle stars,
And the vast world beneath hides him from me!

CLOSED.

The crimson dawn breaks through the clouded east,
And waking breezes round the casement pipe;
They blow the globes of dew from opening buds,
And steal the odors of the sleeping flowers.
The swallow calls its young ones from the eaves,
To dart above their shadows on the lake,
Till its long rollers redden in the sun,
And bend the lances of the mirrored pines.
Who knows the miracle that brings the morn?
Still in my house I linger, though the night—
The night that hides me from myself is gone.
Light robes the world, but strips me bare again.
I will not follow on the paths of day.
I know the dregs within its crystal hours;
The bearers of my cups have served me well;
I drained them, and the bearers come no more.
Rise, morning, rise, for those believing souls
Who seek completion in day's garish light.
My casement I will close, keep shut my door,
Till day and night are only dreams to me.

MEMORY IS IMMORTAL.

Time passed, as passes time with common souls,
Whose thoughts and wishes end with every day;
For whom no future is, whose present hours
Reveal no looming shade of that which was.

But Memory is immortal, for she comes
To me, from heaven or hell, to me, once more!
As birds that migrate choose the ocean wind
That beats them helpless, while it steers them home,
So I was this way driven—I chose this way—
Of old my dwelling-place, where all my race
Are buried. At first I was enchanted here;
Impossible appeared the pall, the shroud;
And in my spell I trod the grassy streets,
Where in the summer days mild oxen drew
The bristling hay, and in the winter snows
The creaking masts and knees for mighty ships,
Whose hulls were parted on the coral reefs,
Or foundered in the depth of Arctic nights.
I wandered through the gardens rank and waste,
Wonderful once, when I was like the flowers;
Along the weedy paths grew roses still,
Surviving empire, but remaining queens.

My mood established by the slumbrous town—
(Slumber with slumber, dream with dream should be)
I sought a mansion on the lonely shore,
From which, his feet made level with his head,
Its occupant was gone. I lived alone.
Whoso, beneath this roof, had played his part
In life's deep tragedy, not here again
Could be rehearsed its scenes of love or hate.
Upon the ancient walls my pictures hung,
Of men and women, strong and beautiful,
Whose shoulders pushed along the world's great wheel;
Landscapes, where cloud and mountain rose as one,

Where rivers crept in secret vales, or rolled
Past city walls, whose towers and palaces
By slaves were builded, and by princes fallen!
And books whose pages ever told one tale,
The tale of human love, in joy or pain,
The seed of our last hope — Eternity.
Days glided by, this mirage cheating all;
Morn came, eve went, and we were tranquil still.
If form, and sound, and color fail to show,
By poet's, painter's, sculptor's noble touch,
The subtle truth of Nature, can I tell
How Nature poised my mind in light and shade?

But Memory is immortal, and to me
She advanced, silent, slow, a muffled shape.
One moonlight night I walked through long white lanes;
The sky and sea were like a frosted web;
The air was heavy with familiar scents,
Which travelled down the wind, I knew from where —
The fragrance of a grove of Northern pines.
My feet were hastening thither — and my heart!
At last I stood before a funeral mound,
From which I fled when vanished love and life —
Long years ago — fled from my father's house;
Banished myself, to banish him I loved —
His broken history and his early grave.
And in the moonlight Memory floated on,
Immortal, with my now immortal Love!

THE TRYST.

Impelled by memory in a wayward mood,
Reluctant, yearning, with a faithless mind,
I sought once more a long neglected spot,
A wooded upland bordered by the sea,
Whose tides were swirling up the reedy sands,

Or floating noiseless in the yellow marsh.
My way was wild. The winds, awaking, smote
My face, but as I passed a ruined wall
Brambles and vines and waving blossoms dashed
A frolic-welcome, like a summer rain.
Shouldering the hills against the murky east
Stood stalwart oaks, and in the mossy sod
Below the trembling birches whispered me,
"Not here!" I reached the silence-loving pines,
And lingered. The mists swept from the wooded hills,
And, rolling seaward, hid the anchored ships.
So, happy, dreaming an old dream again,
Of keeping tryst in secret on the knoll,
I wandered on, listening in dreamy maze
To sounds I thought familiar, — the approach
Of well-known footsteps in the leafy path, —
A murmuring voice calling me by name!
Through the pine shafts the sunless light of dawn
Stole. Day was come. My dream would be fulfilled!
Above the hills the sky began to blaze,
And ushering morn the west flushed rosy-red;
Then, the Sun leaping from his bed of gold,
Scattered cloud-banners, crimson, gray, and white.
There was my shadow in the leafy path
Alone, — none was to keep the tryst with me!
No voice, no step among the hills I heard.
The joyous swallows from their nestlings flew,
Mad in the light with song. Far out at sea
The white sails fluttered in the eager breeze,
But Day was silent holding tryst with me, —
My pilgrimage rewarded — faith restored.

NO ANSWER.

You tell me not, green multitude of leaves,
Mingling and whirling with the willful breeze,

Nor you, bright grasses, trembling blade to blade,
What meaneth June, to hap us every year?

The spirit of the flowers is watching now,
As winking in the sun they suck the dew,
The thickets parley with the splendid fields—
What meaneth June, to hap us every year?

Up where the brook laps round the shining flags,
And tinkling foam bells pass the weedy shore,
And where the willow swings above the trout—
What meaneth June, to hap us every year?

The clouds hold knowledge in their snowy peaks,
They hide it in their moving fleecy folds,
They share it with the sunset's golden isles—
What meaneth June, to hap us every year?

Fullness and sweetness, and the power of life,
Must I in ignorance remain alone,
And yield the quest of speech for certain proof?
What meaneth June, to hap us every year?

Sweetness and beauty, and the power of life,
Is it creation's anthem—parts for all?
Is this the knowledge—will you answer me
What meaneth June, to hap us every year?

ON THE HILLTOP.

"By the margent of the sea
I would build myself a home."

Not by the margent of the sea,
But on the hilltop I would be,

My little house a mossy den,
Between me and the world of men.
Beside me dips a wide ravine,
Covered with a flowery screen;
Far round me rise a band of hills,
Whose voices reach me by their rills,
Or deep susurrus of the wood,
That stands in stately brotherhood,
Upholding one vast web of green,
Whereunder foot has never been—
The pine and elm, the birch and oak—
And thus their voices me invoke:
"If you would on the hilltop be,
We cannot share your misery;
Cease, cease this moaning for the Past:
The law of grief can never last."
When springtime brings anemones,
Upon the sod I take my ease,
Or search for Arethusa's pink,
Along the torrent's ragged brink;
Or in the tinted April hours
I watch the curtain of the showers
That fall beneath a lurking cloud,
Which for a moment throws a shroud
On the sun's arrows in the west,
Till it blaze up a golden crest.
The young moon bends her crescent horn
Against the lingering summer morn;
Then, riding down the starry sky,
She follows me till night goes by.
And when the dawn breaks on yon town,
I think the sleepers lying down
Must rise to shoulder dismal care
Methinks that once was but my fare.
But I upon the hilltop yet
Am free from every tangling fret;
So ever thus, in peace of mind,
I give my pity to my kind.
For me this noble solitude!

And as I face its varying mood,
Reflected in its every show,
Some higher self I come to know.
See, autumn here, with color glad,
Not like the poets—russet clad—
But scarlet, umber, green, and gold;
Then in a breath I must behold
The autumn winds tear down my screen,
And leave me not a leaf to glean.
The snow will cover glen and height,
And all my hilltop glisten white;
I see the crystal atoms fly
Under the dome of this gray sky.
Like gnomes are they, these spectral gleams?
Or shall I guess them only dreams?
Whatever is the truth, I say,
If up and down the world I stray,
Still on the hilltop I would be,
Not by the margent of the sea!

THE MESSAGE.

To you, my comrades, whether far or near,
I send this message. Let our past revive;
Come, sound reveille to our hearts once more.
Expecting, I shall wait till at my door
I see you enter, each and every one
Tumultuous, eager all, with clamorous speech,
To hide my stammering welcome and my tears.
I am no host carousing long and late,
Enticing guests with epicurean hints;
Nor am I Timon, sick of this sad world,
Who, jesting, cries, "The sky is overhead,
And underneath that famous rest, the earth:
Show me the man who can have more at last."

Without, the thunder of the city rolls;
Within, the quiet of the student reigns.
There is a change. Time was a childish voice.
Sweet as the lark's when from her nest she soars,
Thrilled over all, and vanished into heaven.
Music once triumphed here: the skilful hand
Of him who rarely struck the keys, and woke
My soul in harmony grand as his own,
Is folded on his breast, my soldier love.
Here hangs his portrait, under it his sword;
He served his country, and his grave's afar.
Dread not this place as one to relics given,
Though I have decked with amaranth my wall,
The testimony of a later loss —
His who long wandering in foreign lands,
Then dying, crossed the sea to die with me.
Behold the sunrise and the morning clouds
On yonder canvas, misty mountain-peaks —
The simple grandeur of a perfect art!
Behold these vivid woods, that gleam beside
The happy vision of an autumn eve,
When red leaves fall, and redder sunsets fade!
The world grows pensive sinking into night,
Whose melancholy space hides sighing winds:
Can they reply to sadder human speech?
What centuries are counted here — my books!
Shadows of mighty men; the chorus, hark!
The antique chant vibrates, and Fate compels!

Comrades, return; the midnight lamp shall gleam
As in old nights; the chaplets woven then —
Withered, perhaps, by time — may grace us yet;
The laurel faded is the laurel still,
And some of us are heroes to ourselves.
And amber wine shall flow; the blue smoke wreathe
In droll disputes, with metaphysics mixed;
Or float as lightly as the quick-spun verse,
Threading the circle round from thought to thought,
Sparkling and fresh as is the airy web

Spread on the hedge at morn in silver dew.
The scent of roses you remember well;
In the green vases they shall bloom again.
And me — do you remember? I remain
Unchanged, I think; though one I saw like me
Some years ago, with hair that was not white;
And she was with you then, as brave a soul
As souls can be whom Fate has not approached.
But seek and find me now, unchanged or changed,
Mirthful in tears, and in my laughter sad.

EXILE.

Blind in these stony streets, dumb in their crowds,
What can I do but dream of other days?
Whose is the love I had, and have not now?
If it be Nature's, let her answer me.
It wanders by the blue, monotonous sea,
Where rushes grow, or follows all the sweep
Of shallow summer brooks and umber pools.
Or does it linger in those hidden paths
Where starlike blossoms blow among dead leaves,
And dark groves murmur over darker shrubs,
Birds with their fledgelings sleep, and pale moths flit?
With sunset's crimson flags perhaps it goes,
And reappears with yellow Jupiter,
Riding the West beside the crescent moon.
Comes it with sunrise, when the sunrise floats
From Night's bold towers, vast in the East, and gray
Till tower and wall flash into fiery clouds,
Moving along the verge, stately and slow,
Ordered by the old music of the spheres?
Perchance it trembles in October's oaks;
Or, twining with the brilliant, berried vine,
Would hide the tender, melancholy elm.
Well might it rest within those solemn woods

Where sunlight never falls — whose tops are green
With airs from heaven, — its balmy mists and rains, —
While underneath black, mossy, mammoth rocks
Keep silence with the waste of blighted boughs.
If winter riots with the wreathing snow,
And ocean, tossing all his threatening plumes,
And winds, that tear the hollow, murky sky,
Can this, my love, which dwells no more with me,
Find dwelling there, — like some storm-driven bird,
That knows not whence it flew, nor where to fly,
Between the world of sea and world of cloud,
At last drops dead in the remorseless deep?

A SEASIDE IDYL.

I wandered to the shore, nor knew I then
What my desire, — whether for wild lament,
Or sweet regret, to fill the idle pause
Of twilight, melancholy in my house,
And watch the flowing tide, the passing sails,
Or to implore the air, and sea, and sky,
For that eternal passion in their power
Which souls like mine who ponder on their fate
May feel, and be as they — gods to themselves.
Thither I went, whatever was my mood.
The sands, the rocks, and beds of bending sedge,
I saw alone. Between the east and west,
Along the beach no creature moved besides.
High on the eastern point a lighthouse shone;
Steered by its lamp a ship stood out to sea,
And vanished from its rays towards the deep,
While in the west, above a wooded isle,
An island-cloud hung in the emerald sky,
Hiding pale Venus in its sombre shade.
I wandered up and down the sands, I loitered
Among the rocks, and trampled through the sedge:

But I grew weary of the stocks and stones.
"I will go hence," I thought; "the Elements
Have lost their charm; my soul is dead to-night.
Oh passive, creeping Sea, and stagnant Air,
Farewell! Dull sands, and rocks, and sedge, farewell."
Homeward I turned my face, but stayed my feet.
Should I go back but to revive again
The ancient pain? Hark! suddenly there came
From over sea, a sound like that of speech;
And suddenly I felt my pulses leap
As though some Presence were approaching me.
Loud as the voice of Ocean's dark-haired king
A breeze came down the sea, — the sea rose high;
The surging waves sang round me — this their song:
"Oh, yet your love will triumph! He shall come
In love's wild tumult; he shall come once more, —
By tracks of ocean or by paths of earth;
The wanderer will reach you and remain."
The breakers dashed among the rocks, and they
Seemed full of life; the foam dissolved the sands,
And the sedge trembled in the swelling tide.
Was this a promise of the vaunting Sea,
Or the illusion of a last despair?
Either, or both, still homeward I must go,
And that way turned mine eyes, and thought they met
A picture, — surely so, — or I was mad.
The crimson harvest-moon was rising full
Above my roof, and glimmered on my walls.
Within the doorway stood a man I knew —
No picture this. I saw approaching me
Him I had hoped for, grieved for, and despaired.
"My ship is wrecked," he cried, "and I return
Never to leave my love. You are my love?"
"I too am wrecked," I sighed, "by lonely years;
Returning, you but find another wreck."
He bent his face to search my own, and spake:
"What I have traversed sea and land to find,
I find. For liberty I fought, and life,
On savage shores and wastes of unknown seas,

While waiting for this hour. Oh, think you not
Immortal love mates with immortal love
Always? And now, at last, we know this love."
My soul was filling with a mighty joy
I could not show — yet must I show my love.
"From you whose will divided broke our hearts
I now demand a different kiss than that
Which then you said should be our parting kiss.
Given, I vow the past shall be forgot.
The kiss — and we are one! Give me the kiss."
Like the dark rocks upon the sands he stood,
When on his breast I fell, and kissed his lips.
All the wild clangor of the sea was hushed;
The rapid silver waves ran each to each,
Lapsed in the deep with joyous, murmured sighs.
Years of repentance mine, forgiveness his,
To tell. Happy, we paced the tranquil shores,
Till between sea and sky we saw the sun,
And all our wiser, loving days began.

THE CHIMNEY-SWALLOW'S IDYL.

From where I built the nest for my first young,
In the high chimney of this ancient house,
I saw the household fires burn and go down,
And know what was and is forever gone.
My dusky, swift-winged fledgelings, flying far
To seek their mates in clustered eaves or towers,
Would linger not to learn what I have learned,
Soaring through air or steering over sea —
These single, solitary walls must fade.
But I return, inhabiting my nest,
A little simple bird, which still survives
The noble souls now vanished from this hearth;
And none are here besides but she who shares
My life, and pensive vigil holds with me.

No longer does she mourn; she lives serene;
I see her mother's beauty in her face,
I see her father's quiet pride and power,
The linked traits and traces of her race;
Her brothers dying, like strong sapling trees
Hewn down by violent blows prone in dense woods,
Covered with aged boughs, decaying slow.
She muses thus: "Beauty once more abides;
The rude alarm of death, its wild amaze
Is over now. The chance of change has passed;
No doubtful hopes are mine, no restless dread,
No last word to be spoken, kiss to give
And take in passion's agony and end.
They cannot come to me, but in good time
I shall rejoin my silent company,
And melt among them, as the sunset clouds
Melt in gray spaces of the coming night."
So she holds dear as I this tranquil spot,
And all the flowers that blow, and maze of green,
The meadows daisy-full, or brown and sere;
The shore which bounds the waves I love to skim,
And dash my purple wings against the breeze.
When breaks the day I twitter loud and long,
To make her rise and watch the vigorous sun
Come from his sea-bed in the weltering deep,
And smell the dewy grass, still rank with sleep.
I hover through the twilight round her eaves,
And dart above, before her, in her path,
Till, with a smile, she gives me all her mind;
And in the deep of night, lest she be sad
In sleepless thought, I stir me in my nest,
And murmur as I murmur to my young;
She makes no answer, but I know she hears;
And all the cherished pictures in her thoughts
Grow bright because of *me*, her swallow friend!

LAST DAYS.

As one who follows a departing friend,
Destined to cross the great, dividing sea,
I watch and follow these departing days,
That go so grandly, lifting up their crowns
Still regal, though their victor Autumn comes.
Gifts they bestow, which I accept, return,
As gifts exchanged between a loving pair,
Who may possess them as memorials
Of pleasures ended by the shadow — Death.
What matter which shall vanish hence, if both
Are transitory — me, and these bright hours —
And of the future ignorant alike?
From all our social thralls I would be free.
Let care go down the wind — as hounds afar,
Within their kennels baying unseen foes,
Give to calm sleepers only calmer dreams.
Here will I rest alone: the morning mist
Conceals no form but mine; the evening dew
Freshens but faded flowers and my worn face.
When the noon basks among the wooded hills
I too will bask, as silent as the air
So thick with sun-motes, dyed like yellow gold,
Or colored purple like an unplucked plum.
The thrush, now lonesome, for her young have flown,
May flutter her brown wings across my path;
And creatures of the sod with brilliant eyes
May leap beside me, and familiar grow.
The moon shall rise among her floating clouds,
Black, vaporous fans, and crinkled globes of pearl,
And her sweet silver light be given to me.
To watch and follow these departing days
Must be my choice; and let me mated be
With Solitude; may memory and hope
Unite to give me faith that nothing dies;
To show me always, what I pray to know,
That man alone may speak the word — *Farewell.*